THE STARTLING STORY
OF THE STOLEN STATUE

#2

THE STARTLING STORY OF THE STOLEN STATUE

by Tony Abbott

illustrated by Colleen Madden

EGMONT
New York USA

EGMONT

We bring stories to life

First published by Egmont USA, 2012
443 Park Avenue South, Suite 806
New York, NY 10016

Text copyright © Tony Abbott, 2012
Illustrations copyright © Colleen Madden, 2012
All rights reserved

1 3 5 7 9 8 6 4 2

www.egmontusa.com
www.tonyabbottbooks.com
www.greenfrographics.com

Library of Congress Cataloging-in-Publication Data
Abbott, Tony.
The startling story of the stolen statue / by Tony Abbott ;
illustrated by Colleen Madden.
p. cm. -- (Goofballs ; 2)
Summary: As Badger Point School is preparing to celebrate its
100th anniversary, the statue of its founder, Simon Plunkett, goes
missing but the Goofballs are quickly on the case, looking for
evidence and following clues.
ISBN 978-1-60684-165-5 (hardcover) -- ISBN 978-1-60684-341-3
(pbk.) -- ISBN 978-1-60684-299-7 (ebook) [1. Mystery and detective
stories. 2. Stealing--Fiction. 3. Statues--Fiction. 4. Schools--
Fiction. 5. Anniversaries--Fiction.] I. Madden, Colleen, ill. II.
Title.
PZ7.A1587St 2012
[Fic]--dc23
2011025299

Printed in the United States of America

Book design by Alison Chamberlain

To Dolores, who keeps me laughing.

—T.A.

Contents

1

Good News, Bad News

My name is Jeff Bunter, and I'm the chief, first, and number one Goofball on the planet.

My best friends, Brian Rooney, Kelly Smitts, and Mara Lubin, are the other Goofballs.

They're also on the planet (except it's sometimes hard to tell with Brian).

Together, we solve mysteries.

Goofball mysteries.

Like the one yesterday. It was huge. You could even call it the Crime of the Century!

And it all happened at our school.

It was also our goofiest mystery so far. There was a smelly scrap of paper. A word too long to say. A chunk of cheese. A pet badger. And Brian's favorite pants.

But hold on. I'm getting ahead of myself.

Which can hurt. Because when I stop, Brian, Kelly, and Mara bump into me, and we all end up on the floor like a pile of sandbags.

Oh, right. Sandbags.

They were part of the mystery, too.

So let me begin at the beginning. Or rather at the end. The end of the school day.

Because that's when the mystery started.

We were all in homeroom, talking about the huge party that evening.

Badger Point School was having its 100th anniversary. A statue of the school's first principal would be unveiled. Because we had no mystery to solve, the other Goofballs and I had spent the whole week putting up decorations.

All of a sudden—*Krrkkkk! Pppppp! Zzzzzt!*

No, it wasn't Mara blowing her nose.

It was the public-address system, making noise like firecrackers exploding in a radio. Trust me, I know what that sounds like. Brian did that once.

When the crackling ended, everyone hushed. Then came the announcement.

"Jeff Bunter, Brian Rooney, Kelly Smitts, and Mara Lubin, please report after school to the Cafeteri-Audi-Nasium!"

Because Badger Point is a small school, they combined the cafeteria, the auditorium, and the gymnasium into one room. They even give golf lessons to grown-ups there on Saturdays. That's a long list of stuff to do in one room, so they had to find a long name for it.

Cafeteri-Audi-Nasium!

It's where the big party was going to be.

Kelly twirled her blond curls. "I wonder if we need to put up more decorations."

"Or test the refreshments!" said Mara, who loves to eat but is as skinny as a stick.

BRRRRRNG! The dismissal bell rang. The halls filled with kids racing out of school, and the four of us headed down to the big room.

Banners were hung on the walls of the hallways. Streamers in purple and white, the school colors, hung from the ceiling.

"Don't get me wrong," said Kelly. "I love parties. But it's been days since our last mystery. My detection skills are getting rusty."

"I hardly feel goofy anymore!" said Brian.

"You still look pretty goofy," said Mara.

Brian grinned. "Thanks. I try."

My heart skipped. "What if we're being called to the Cafeteri-Audi-Nasium to solve a mystery? My cluebook is totally ready!"

My cluebook is what I call a small notebook I carry with me everywhere. I write down anything that looks, smells, sounds, feels, or tastes like a clue. Private detectives do this all the time. It helps us solve mysteries.

"If it's a mystery, I can use my cool stuff," said Brian, patting his bulging pockets.

Because Brian is an inventor, his pockets are always packed with weird junk. Too bad his mystery-solving inventions never really work.

"We can wear new disguises!" said Mara.

garbage twisty ties

pom-poms

Legos

First-aid tape

plastic sandwich bag

refrigerator magnets

plastic screw

dog kibble

measuring tape

Mara is the queen of goofy disguises. On our last case, we dressed up as plants. Before that, we were lumps of pizza dough. Before that, we were big fluffy rats. We'll dress up as anything to solve a mystery.

The school was pretty empty by the time we entered the final corridor. Then we saw Billy Carlson, a boy from our homeroom. He was picking something up from the floor.

"Hey, Billy," said Kelly.

"It's not me," he said. Then he ran as fast as he could down the hall the opposite way.

"*That* was mysterious," whispered Kelly.

"And I'm writing it down," I said.

Saw Billy Carlson in hall.
"It's not me," he said.

We turned one last corner, and there it was.

The Cafeteri-Audi-Nasium.

It was the biggest room in the school. It had everything—basketball nets, climbing ropes, bleachers, and cafeteria tables.

It even had a ramp up to a stage. But when we stepped in, we knew something wasn't right.

Kelly froze. "A man is *lurking* behind the curtain! *He* did it!" she whispered.

We didn't know if *anyone* had done *anything* yet, but Kelly was right about one thing. A man *was* lurking behind the curtain.

Lurking is a detective word. You use it to describe someone who looks like he is sneaking around. And Kelly thinks pretty much everybody looks sneaky. She's not always right. But she is great at solving mysteries.

I wrote it down.

Man lurking onstage

"Sneak up on him," I said. "Be stealthy."

Stealthy is another detective word. It means silent and careful. But I guess Brian was out the day we learned that word. Because he tripped on his shoelaces and fell with a thud.

"What—?" the lurking man said with a gasp.

"What—?" we gasped back.

2

A Stack of Clues

"Principal Higgins?" I said to the man lurking behind the curtain.

"Shhh!" whispered Principal Higgins, his face wrinkled in a frown. "I'm hiding!"

"But we see you right there," said Kelly.

"I'm not hiding from *you*," he said.

We went totally quiet. No one breathed. No one moved. Finally, the principal's shoulders sank and he sighed a big sigh. "Oh, dear . . ."

"Sir," said Mara, "please tell us—*in your own words*—exactly what's wrong."

Principal Higgins sighed again. "It's a calamity, a misadventure of cataclysmic proportions, a tragic and devastating debacle—"

The thing with Principal Higgins is that his own words are not the same as our own words.

But one thing I *did* understand. Principal Higgins was upset. "Excuse me, sir," I said. "Tell us what's wrong—in *normal* words."

I had my cluebook open and ready.

Principal Higgins drew the curtain and crossed the stage to a tall shape covered with a white cloth. "You know that Simon Plunkett was Badger Point School's first principal one century ago?" he asked.

"Yes, sir," said Mara. "The anniversary party tonight is all about Simon Plunkett. We can't wait to see the new statue of him!"

Principal Higgins frowned. "This afternoon was very busy for me," he said. "A student asked to leave early. I had to count the special gifts to be given out to everyone tonight. I ordered the refreshments. Mrs. Bookman, the librarian, brought me a book. I had to write my speech. A thousand things—"

"Wait!" I said, scribbling all that down.

Student leaving school early
Special gifts
Mrs. Bookman brings a book

"Okay, go on," I said.

The principal put his hand on the cloth. "But when I came to make sure that the new statue was ready, look what I found!"

He pulled the cloth away, and the "statue" looked just like a pile of chairs stacked up on each other as tall as a person.

"Chairs?" said Mara. "Simon Plunkett was a bunch of *chairs*?"

"Of course not," Principal Higgins said.

"Did he *invent* chairs?" Brian asked.

"No, no, you're not following me," the principal said.

"You're not going anywhere," said Kelly.

Principal Higgins shut his eyes and got red in the face. "What I am trying to say is that the statue of our first principal, Principal Plunkett, the statue to be unveiled at our celebration tonight—has been *stolen!*"

We all gasped.

Then I wrote it down.

Stage
Statue
Stolen!

Of course, *stolen* is one of the most important detective words of all. Many times it's the reason there is a mystery in the first place.

"This crime," said the principal, "is the worst thing that has happened at Badger Point School in one hundred years."

"It's the Crime of the Century!" said Brian.

"It is!" said the principal. "And now I must cancel the party and call the police! I wanted to tell you first, since you were in charge of all the wonderful decorations."

I felt dizzy. "No!" I said.

"I have no choice," he said. "We have only two hours before the celebration, and our statue has vanished without a trace!"

And that's the difference between normal people and Goofballs.

"There is *always* a trace," I said slowly.

"And we'll find that trace," said Mara. "Let *us* find the statue. We can do it. Please?"

"You? Oh, I don't know . . . ," he started.

"Sir," Kelly began, "the Goofballs are famous. We ended the Totally Incredible Pizza Disaster. We found Randall Crandall's missing pony. We figured out who threw the Flying First Grader. We even solved the case of the stolen statue! Oh, wait. That's *this* case. But we *will* solve it, I promise!"

SOLVED!

SOLVED!

SOLVED!

"We all promise!" said Mara.

Principal Higgins looked doubtful.

"Sir," I said, "this is a job for the experts."

"But I thought it was a job for us," said Brian.

I looked at him.

"Oh, wait. We *are* the experts."

Principal Higgins paced the stage. He looked at the chairs, then out at the empty Cafeteri-Audi-Nasium. Finally, he said, "I suppose two hours won't make a difference. Go ahead. Do your Goofball best."

I started to write that in my cluebook when footsteps squeaked suddenly behind us.

Kelly spun around. "*He* did it!" she cried, even before seeing who it was.

But it was only the custodian,
Mr. Wick.

Except that *only* is wrong, because
Mr. Wick does way more than clean.
He teaches art. He coaches sports. He
drives a bus. He cooks in the kitchen.
He even directs school shows.

Maybe *he* should have a longer name,
too!

Like Mr.Wickercleanerteachercooker-drivercoach!

"I just came to say that I found a visitor scratching to get in," Mr. Wick said, and a dog with tall ears and no tail galloped over.

"Sparky!" I said. "Come here, boy!"

Sparky is my corgi, the official Goofdog and a valued member of our mystery-solving team.

"A dog in our school?" asked the principal.

"He's part of the Goofball crew," I told him.

"Goof! Goof!" Sparky barked.

Principal Higgins sighed one last time. "I'll call your parents and tell them you are here."

Then he left the room with Mr. Wick.

"If we solve an official school mystery, our fame will spread everywhere!" said Kelly.

"Like warm peanut butter," added Mara.

I stepped to the podium and tapped the microphone. "Goofballs, your attention, please. You know the drill. What's first?"

"First, we each take a wall!" said Mara.

"Second, we put our noses to the floor!" said Brian.

"Third, we hope there's nothing stinky down there," said Kelly as she watched Brian unfold a "laser" helmet of earmuffs, tiny mirrors, and a scuba mask with no glass in it.

I nodded. "And what's fourth?"

Everyone was too busy gawking at Brian's goofy invention to answer.

"Goofballs!" I cried. "I said, *what's fourth*?"

"We search for clues!" they all said.

And that's just what we did.

3

The Cafeteri-Audi-Nasium!

While solving our last few mysteries, the Goofballs have developed a system for finding clues. It's called THE GOOFBALL SYSTEM FOR FINDING CLUES.

Mara took the north wall of the room. Kelly took the south wall. I took the east wall. Brian took the west wall. Sparky took the middle.

"Ready?" I said. "Begin!"

It must have looked like a really silly dance, but it's how Goofballs solve cases.

Mara was down on her hands and knees, staring through her green-rimmed glasses.

Kelly power walked in super-slow motion over every inch of her part of the room, her eyes as wide as a couple of searchlights.

Brian zigzagged along his wall, three steps away, three steps back, scanning the floor through his laser helmet like an alien detective.

I was bent in half, creeping along with baby steps, my nose grazing the floor, my cluebook ready for any clue I could find.

If *some* private eyes know something about everything, and *other* private eyes know everything about something, the *Goofballs* know a few things about a few things.

But it totally worked, because after a few minutes of THE GOOFBALL SYSTEM FOR FINDING CLUES, we found our first clue.

To be exact, *I* found the first clue. By accident. The kind of accident where somebody gets hurt. Me!

I was turning away from my first corner when suddenly—*sloop! wham!*—my feet were in the air and my back was on the floor!

"Hey! Who tripped me?" I cried.

"Your feet did," Brian said through his scuba mask.

"No, they didn't," I said. "*That* did!"

As everyone ran over, I picked up a very short stub of a broken pencil. It was the pointed end and only three inches long. Besides that, it was gold and looked brand-new.

"Wait. A pencil?" asked Brian. "*That's* what tripped you?"

"A *broken* pencil," I said, sniffing the broken end. "And judging by the fresh smell of the wood, this pencil was broken very recently."

Mara blinked through her glasses. "What's so important about a broken pencil?"

I grinned, knowing what I would say. "Maybe nothing . . . maybe everything."

"Good line," said Kelly. "Write it, Jeff."

I like good lines, so I did.

Broken pencil
Maybe nothing
Maybe everything

Kelly frowned. "But how do we solve the mystery if all we have is a pencil stub?"

"We think," said Mara. "So I'll play some thinking music." She sat down at the piano.

"I didn't know you played piano," said Brian.

"I don't," Mara said. "Ready?"

Before we could say "No," Mara
raised her fingers and dropped them
hard on the keys.

*BLOINKKKK! Blinkety-plonkety-
thung!*

Mara blinked. "I know I can't play,
but no one's *this* bad." She flipped up
the top of the piano and looked in.
"Well, of all the goofy things. . . . Kelly,
hold my feet. I'm going in!"

Mara disappeared into the top of the piano while Kelly held her feet.

"I did that once," said Brian.

"Went into a piano?" I asked.

"No. Held someone's feet," he said.

"Whose?" I asked.

"Mine," he said. "I was a baby at the time."

"On this planet?" I asked.

"I'm pretty sure."

"Hoist me up, Kelly!" cried Mara.

Kelly pulled and pulled, and when Mara came up, she wasn't empty-handed. Clasped in her hands was a purple board with wheels on it.

"Clue number two," Mara said.
"A skateboard hidden in the piano."

"Not the usual place to hide a skateboard," said Brian. "But good to know."

"Clue three!" cried Kelly, spotting something and running across the stage to it.

"It's a torn slip of paper," she said, sniffing it. "It smells strange, for one thing, and it's damp and ripped, but you can still read it."

We all looked and made out some
letters.

HEES
GRATE

Brian gasped. *"Hees grate?* Why
would the thief write about me? What
could it possibly mean?"

"That you spell as bad as the thief
does," I said. "Let's look for clues in the
hall."

"I don't have my clue from here
yet," said Brian. "I'll keep looking. You
go on ahead."

"Go on a head? We're not hats," said
Kelly.

Brian laughed. "Good joke."

Kelly frowned. "Who's joking? We're *not* hats." Which is another thing about Kelly. Sometimes she only sees what's there and doesn't get the joke. But not getting the joke is sometimes the goofiest thing there is!

We left Brian and Sparky sniffing around the Cafeteri-Audi-Nasium. Well, Sparky was sniffing. Brian was staring up at the climbing ropes hanging from the ceiling.

"Goofballs," I said when we stepped into the hallway, "so far, we have a broken pencil, a skateboard, and a smelly slip of paper with letters on it. What do these clues tell us?"

"That we need more clues?" said Mara.

"Or we need to know more about the clues we *do* have," said Kelly, sniffing the paper. "This paper smells like something—"

Suddenly, there came a loud cry from the Cafeteri-Audi-Nasium. "Help!"

Mara, Kelly, and I stared at one another.

"That's Brian!" I cried. "He's in trouble!"

4

Rooney the Loony

We raced back into the Cafeteri-Audi-Nasium, expecting to find Brian held prisoner by the statue thief. Instead, we found Brian held prisoner by the climbing ropes.

He was hanging halfway up and was as tangled as Kelly's extra-curly blond hair when it's windy.

Plus he had no pants on.

"Brian, get down from there!" said Mara.

"Give me my cargo shorts first!" Brian yelled.

"Why didn't you keep them with you?" asked Kelly.

"They're so heavy with invention stuff, they slipped off," he said.

Sparky was dragging Brian's cargo shorts around the room. I cornered him and got them back, then tossed them up to Brian. It was amazing how he put them on with one hand. Then he reached up and unhooked the rope next to his and slid to the floor.

"Why were you up there?" asked Kelly.

Brian held the second climbing rope loosely in his hand. "I saw something up there."

"We saw something up there, too," Mara told him. "And we wish we didn't."

"But this rope was hooked to the ceiling differently from the others," Brian said. "And because of it, I know without a shadow of a doubt that our thief is a very rich man with bushy red hair and a tiny pet monkey!"

We stared at Brian.

"How do you figure all that?" Kelly asked. "And so quickly?"

Brian smiled. "Simple logic. Clues, please."

We gave them to him.

"First of all," he said, "only a rich man would have golden pencils. He used one to keep the Cafeteri-Audi-Nasium door open while he did his stealing. . . ."

I nodded slowly. "The pencil in the door makes sense, but the pencil's not real gold, you know."

"Let me finish," Brian said. "Second, everyone knows that rich men drive fancy cars. But you can't drive cars in school, so naturally he would bring a skateboard."

"Wait. Is that logical?" asked Mara.

"But there's more!" Brian said. "Because the thief didn't want his fancy clothes messed up, he must have had a pet monkey, which he sent up one of the climbing ropes to unhook the one next to it. Just like I did."

"But—" Kelly said.

"There's even more!" said Brian. "Sparky, you be the statue."

Sparky ran up onstage and stood very still.

Brian smiled. "Our thief lifted the statue from the stage onto the skateboard." Brian lifted Sparky onto the skateboard. "Then the monkey used his tiny little fingers to tie the climbing rope to the skateboard. Together, they rolled the statue from the Cafeteri-Audi-Nasium stage, down the Cafeteri-Audi-Nasium ramp, and out the Cafeteri-Audi-Nasium door, which closed behind the thieves, breaking the gold pencil and sending it spinning across the Cafeteri-Audi-Nasium—"

"Stop!" cried Kelly. "Cafeteri-Audi-Nasium takes too long to say!"

"And takes up too much space in my head," said Mara.

"And in my cluebook," I said. "How about just . . . Caf?"

"Agreed!" everyone said.

"But how in the world do you know the thief has bushy red hair?" Mara asked.

Brian grinned. "For the simple reason that I don't know anyone with bushy red hair. I *also* don't know any very rich men. It follows logically that a very rich man *must* have bushy red hair." I was about to object when Kelly stomped her feet. "But what about *my* clue? What about the smelly paper?"

"That's easy," said Brian. "The paper says HEES GRATE. And now I'll prove that I am. Because here comes my best idea. Since Mara found the skateboard *in* the piano, I believe our rich thief is coming back for it. And I know the perfect way to catch him!"

Without a word, Brian went behind the curtain and came back with two buckets.

"What's in those buckets?" asked Kelly.

Brian placed one bucket next to each of the two doors into the Caf, then turned and smiled.

"Golf balls!" he said. "The plastic ones they use for lessons. When our thief returns to the scene of the crime, he'll knock over the buckets, fall on the golf balls, and we'll catch him!"

"Brian," I said, "I don't know if your solution to the mystery really works—"

All at once, Kelly gasped. She waved the crinkled paper in the air. "I know what this paper smells like! It smells like chlorine!"

"Chlorine?" said Mara. "The blond girl in homeroom? She does have a strange smell."

"No," said Brian, "Chlorine is the girl with pink hair in the first row of math class."

"I think that's violet," I said.

"I thought Violet sat behind Chlorine," said Mara.

"I mean Chlorine's hair is violet," I said.

"Then who's the blonde?" asked Brian.

"Cut—it—out!" shouted Kelly, looking ready to explode. "What I mean is, this paper smells like the *chemical* called *chlorine* in the swimming pool."

Brian shook his head. "She shouldn't be in the pool when school is closed—"

"*Which means*," Kelly continued, glaring at Brian, "that this paper has been *in or near the pool.* Which means that the thief may have left clues there. We need to go there right now!"

"Goof! Goof!" Sparky barked.

Kelly power walked around a bucket of golf balls and straight out of the Caf, her arms flying like a couple of propellers. We followed her down the hall. But our arms were regular.

On our way to the pool, Brian nudged me. "Next time I lose my pants, I'm going in there."

I looked across at the boys' locker room. "Are you *planning* to lose your pants again?"

He shrugged. "You never know. But they have lots of extra clothes in the locker room."

I blinked. "That's the second time you've made sense today, Brian."

He grinned. "It's kind of my limit."

Suddenly, we heard a splash coming from the swimming pool: *Splash!*

Then another: *Splash!*

And another: *Splash!*

Kelly screeched to a stop, her crazy arms frozen in midair.

"The statue stealer!" she whispered.
"He's in the swimming pool!"

5

Water, Water . . .

As we tiptoed down the hall to the pool, my heart was going a mile a minute. But my feet were going an inch a minute. They knew I didn't want to be near the pool or hear any more spooky splashing. No such luck.

Splash!

"The thief is *so* in there," whispered Kelly, her fingers nervously twisting her blond curls.

"I hope it's not that monkey," Brian whispered. "Or Violet. Her pink hair really wigs me out."

"We need disguises," whispered Mara. "What do they have lots of at pools?"

"Water?"

"Diving boards?"

"Slippery tiles?"

"I was thinking of towels," said Mara. "If we wrap up in towels, the thief can't identify us. Plus we won't get wet. Plus-plus we'll be like fluffy bunnies, which is always good."

Everything Mara said was true, so we snuck into the supply room and wrapped ourselves in towels so that the thief couldn't identify us. We were so chubby with towels, we could barely identify ourselves!

We tried to wrap Sparky in towels,
but he just growled at us and ran away.

"When we solve the case, he'll be
back to claim his share of the glory,"
Brian said.

"Or his share of your pants," I said.

Suddenly, we heard footsteps sloshing in the next room and a door banging closed.

"We've trapped him!" said Mara.

"Be stealthy," I whispered. "Brian?"

"I know what it means now," he said.

I waddled up to the door to the swimming pool. I pushed it open. The room was empty, but we saw wet spots in the shape of shoes. They seemed to lead from the pool to a closed door behind the diving board.

Kelly pointed to the door. "He's in there!"

Wiggling his head out of his towel disguise, Brian leaned close to us. "I lost my shoes in that room once. I got to know it backward and forward. I'll surprise the thief."

"Did you ever find your shoes?" I asked.

He shrugged. "It turned out they were on my feet the whole time. Now, hold my climbing rope. I'm going in!"

Brian tiptoed to the door, threw it open, cried, "Aha!"—then leaped into the room, slamming the door shut behind him.

A loud fight broke out. It sounded like furniture cracking and people groaning and something being thrown against the door.

"Take—*that*!" cried Brian. "And *that*!"

There was a loud squeak, and water streamed out from under the door.

"Where is the thief?" asked Kelly.

Brian picked himself up and looked into the room. "He escaped! Which never would have happened if he'd stepped on golf balls!"

"Wait. You *saw* the thief?" Mara asked.

"It was too dark," Brian said. "But he attacked me with mops and junk. Then he turned on the faucet and tried to drown me!"

"The thief turned on the faucet?" I asked.

"And broke it in half," said Brian, holding a piece of faucet in his hand.

Kelly peeked in the empty room. "But this is the only door. And there's no one in there."

"Help!" Brian cried, falling out the door, soaking wet, with his towel disguise falling off. With him came a bunch of mops and brooms and other stuff. Water was spraying all over the floor from a broken faucet.

"Sure, now," said Brian. "But I fought him pretty good."

"Brian?" I said.

"Yes?" he said.

"Did you maybe fight the *mops*?" I asked. "And maybe *you* broke the faucet?"

He looked at me, at the faucet in his hand, at the mops, and at the water gushing from the open pipe. "It may have happened that way. But in my defense, it was really dark."

Kelly sighed. "So the footprints didn't lead *to* the closet. They led *away* from it, to the door to the hallway."

"What do they keep in that closet besides brooms and mops?" asked Mara.

"You mean now?" said Brian, tying the climbing rope around his waist to hold his soggy pants up. "Mostly water."

Then something gold floated past my feet. I snatched it up. "The other half of the broken pencil!" I pulled out the stub of pencil I had found in the Caf. I fitted them together.

"A perfect match!" I said.

Now I could read words on the pencil.

CELEBRATE 100 YEARS OF
BADGER POINT SCHOOL

My whole body began to shake.

I flipped open my cluebook and found what I was looking for. "Ah . . . haaa!"

"Bless you," said Kelly. "If that was a sneeze."

"It wasn't, but thank you," I said. "Goofballs, listen. This pencil isn't from a very rich man. In fact, there's only one place in the whole world to find a pencil like this!"

"The Pencil Association?" said Mara.

"The Museum of Writing Stuff?" said Kelly.

"The Pencils R Us Superstore?" said Brian.

"No, no, and no," I said. "I'll bet anything that this pencil is the special gift Principal Higgins was planning to give out tonight. If it is, and if the thief had one, the thief must have been in the principal's office. So the office is where we need to go right now. Come on!"

"What about the water leak?" asked Mara. "Should we tell Mr. Wick?"

"We're hot on the trail of the thief," I said. "There's no time."

"Besides, what's a little drip when you're solving the Crime of the Century?" said Brian as he quietly closed the closet door.

"Goofballs, to the office!" I cried.

6

In the Office of Principal H.

Tearing off our towel disguises, we raced down the hall. The water seemed to follow us. We slid into the principal's office.

The water followed us there, too.

The office was empty. The desk was clear except for two things. A big, crusty orange book. And a big carton of gold pencils exactly like the broken one.

"I knew it!" I said. "The thief was in this office. We are close to solving this mystery."

"I think we're so close," said Mara, blinking through her big green glasses, "that my lenses are fogging up!"

All at once, we heard footsteps outside the office. My heart skipped a beat.

"Take cover!" I said. "Under the desk!"

"Wait!" said Kelly. "Didn't we hide under a desk once, and didn't we say we'd never do it again?"

"Ah!" I said. "The Ridiculous Riddle of the Dusty Desk. One of our first mysteries. But I don't remember why we said that."

"I think I blocked it out," said Brian.

Footsteps were coming closer.

"Does anyone have a better idea?" I asked.

Stomp! Stomp!

"Under the desk!" they all said.

But the instant we piled under the desk, we *all* remembered why we said we'd never hide under one again.

Even without Sparky, there was room for only one medium-size person under there. Or two tiny people. Or one tiny person and a medium skateboard. Or a medium climbing rope and one small person. But not four medium people, a purple skateboard, a thick climbing rope, two halves of a pencil, the best cluebook ever, and a smelly slip of paper.

Brian's foot was wedged against my chin. My shoulders were in Kelly's and Mara's ears. Someone's knee was squishing my behind.

We were about to explode into a hundred pieces when the office door squeaked open and someone stepped in.

Squish-squish!

A person with wet shoes!
Squish-squish . . . squish-squish!
Two people with wet shoes!
Two thieves?

We heard heavy breathing. The two
thieves were only inches away from us.

They knew what *stealthy* meant. They didn't speak. The next thing I saw was light from a flashlight scanning the top of the desk.

I wiggled my arms and legs to alert the Goofballs to do something we learned on a case last summer.

We were all stuck in a place where we had to talk without anyone hearing us. So we learned to read each other's lips.

Here's how you do it.

You form words *very carefully* on your lips. And you "say" them very s—l—o—w—l—y, moving your lips and tongue in a BIG way. But you don't use your breath to make sound. That way you can be silent and still understand each other.

I wrote all about it in my cluebook. We call it Silent Speak. It's one of the finest of the many fine Goofball detective techniques.

Even as the two thieves searched the desk we were hiding under, we each shifted our eyes so we could all see everyone else's lips.

Our Silent Speak conversation went like this:

"Who can see what's going on?"

"Not me. Can you?"

"No. But I think I smell stinky feet."

"You hope it's only stinky feet."

"A bony elbow is in my face."

"So that's where my elbow is!"

"I can't even feel my elbow."

"I can't feel my face! Or my toes."

"I feel my toes. But someone's licking them."

"Mine too! I really hope it's Sparky."

"Sparky ran away, remember?"

"Then I think I'm going to barf!"

"Go ahead. It already smells like stinky feet."

All of a sudden, one of the thieves sneezed. Then something fell to the floor next to me.

"A piece of cheese!" I mouthed.

"Swiss?" mouthed Mara.

"Looks like cheddar," I answered.

"Never mind the cheese," said a gruff voice. "I have what I came for. The last piece of the puzzle. Come on. We have to get rolling."

"Rolling? Good one, Gramps."

"Gramps? Did you hear that?"

"I have cramps in my knees!"

The four shoes turned and squished out of the room. The door closed behind them.

We untangled ourselves.

"There are *two* of them!" said Kelly.

"One kid and one grandpa!" I said.

"And neither of them sounds like a monkey!" said Brian.

Then Mara snatched up the cheese from the floor. She studied it through her big green glasses. *"This cheese has marks on it,"* she mouthed. *"Not teeth marks. These marks were made by . . . a cheese grater. It all makes sense!"*

"Yes!" said Brian. "Wait. It does? How?"

"*Don't you get it?*" Mara mouthed.
"*It's what's on Kelly's torn paper.*
HEES GRATE. *Add a* C, *an* E, *and
an* R, *and you get* CHEESE
GRATER."

"Brilliant!" I said.

Kelly pointed at the desk. "The big orange book is gone. The thieves stole that, too!"

"Also brilliant," Mara mouthed.

"Mara," said Brian, "you can say your words out loud now. The thieves are gone."

"But this is so much fun!" she mouthed.

7

Kicking the Bucket

When we left Principal Higgins's office, the hall outside was empty and wetter than ever.

"Brian, your leak has spread," said Kelly.

"When did it become *my* leak?" he asked.

"When you broke the faucet," I said.

"Oh," he said. "Did I say it was dark in that closet?"

All of a sudden, footsteps splashed down the hall behind us. We heard heavy breathing.

"They're after us!" cried Mara. "Run!"

Kelly and Mara went flying down one hall. Brian and I raced down another hall. The footsteps followed us. They were getting closer, closer. Then our pursuer cried out.

"Goof!"

We looked around. "It's Sparky!" I said.

But we weren't watching where we were going. A dry patch sent Brian and me skidding right through the doors of the Cafeteri-Audi-Nasium. And into a bucket of golf balls.

CRASH!

We hit the floor like a couple of sandbags.

"It worked!" said Brian. "My trap worked!"

"It wasn't supposed to work on us," I said.

Then Sparky leaped out of the darkness.

I heard something rip, and he raced away.

Brian jumped up and glanced down. "My pants are gone again. Will you look at that?"

"I don't want to," I said. "Let's hurry and find a locker room to get you a new pair."

Brian nodded. "That's always been my plan."

We made our way quickly to the first locker room we passed. Brian dashed in, and I paced the hall. I thought and thought, trying to solve the mystery, but Brian distracted me.

He came out of the locker room wearing a pink T-shirt around his middle, with his legs poking out of the sleeves.

"That looks like a diaper," I said.

Brian tied the climbing rope around his waist. "I prefer to think of them as T-pants."

"They're not even your size," I said.

"I don't care for the color, either," he said.

Then I saw the sign over the door. "That's because you went into the girls' locker room."

Brian frowned. "That explains so much."

Three minutes later, we found the girls. They were completely soaked with water.

"We stopped the leak," said Kelly. Then she gasped. "Brian, are you wearing a diaper?"

Mara stared through her big green glasses. "That's *my* diaper! I mean, my T-shirt!"

Brian hung his head. "You want it back?"

"No, thank you!" said Mara.

"Listen, Goofballs," I said.

"Remember what the grandpa said? *The last piece of the puzzle.* What if we have all the pieces, but they aren't fitting together? Why a cheese grater? What was in the orange book? To solve this mystery, we need to add up our clues."

"Please, no math," Brian said. "I'm upset."

"Because you have no pants?" asked Kelly.

"Because we're not solving this mystery," Brian said. "Because time is running out. Because we're detectives, but we have no thief, no statue, no solution, no pants, no nothing. We *need* to solve this!"

Which proved to me that Brian was a Goofball through and through. So I quickly reread my cluebook, and two clues popped out.

Student leaving school early
Mrs. Bookman brings a book

My brain turned over like a kid who can't sleep the night before a big test. Then it came to me. "I need to use the phone. Come on!"

We made our way quickly to the school phone. I dialed a number I knew by heart.

"Hello," said a voice at the other end. "Children's library, Mrs. Bookman speaking."

"Jeff Bunter here," I said. "The Goofballs are on a case, and we need your help."

"How exciting," she said. "Ask away!"

"You delivered a book to Principal Higgins this afternoon. Can you tell me what it was?"

"I can, and it's not a library book but one of my own," Mrs. Bookman said. "It's called *The History of Badger Point School*."

My heart pounded. "And did you happen to see a student asking to leave early?"

"I did!" Mrs. Bookman said. She told me the student's name, then I thanked her and hung up.

"It's time to unite the Goofball team," I said. "Cover your ears." They did, and at the top of my lungs, I yelled, "SPARKY!"

A minute later, Sparky galloped down the hall, dragging the shreds of Brian's pants.

Brian tied what was left of them on, using the climbing rope as an emergency belt.

"Sparky," I said, "you've been running loose all over the school, haven't you?"

Sparky lowered both ears.

"Did you see the thieves?" Kelly asked.

One of his ears sprang straight up.

"Did you see the statue?" Mara asked.

Sparky's other ear sprang up.

I laughed. "That's it! Sparky, take us to the thieves! And Goofballs, let's find that statue!"

Sparky raced off, and we charged after him, slipping through nearly every corner in the school until we were back at the very scene of the crime. The Cafeteri-Audi-Nasium!

The curtain was down. The stage was dark. But we saw two figures lurking backstage.

Then Kelly clicked on the lights!

"The statue stealers!" I cried. "I knew it!"

A cheese grater fell to the floor. An orange book, too. Two faces gaped at us.

"Please, we can explain!" said one thief.

And when they did, the whole puzzle fell into place. A moment later, the bell rang. The school opened. Crowds squished through the wet halls to the Cafeteri-Audi-Nasium.

The celebration was about to begin!

The Case Is Solved!

Mara and Kelly stayed behind the curtain. Brian and I stood on the stage, facing a room jammed with students, parents, teachers, and practically the whole town.

Principal Higgins walked to the podium.

"Thank you for coming to celebrate a century of Badger Point School," he said. "But I regret to inform you that there will be no—"

"Excuse me, sir," I said, walking up to the podium. "May the Goofballs take over?"

"Well . . . I . . ."

"Brian, the curtain, please," I said.

Brian pulled the rope, and the curtain went up, revealing Kelly and Mara next to a big cloth-covered thing. It looked the same as it had when Principal Higgins showed it to us.

"Goofballs, the cloth, please," I said.

Principal Higgins gasped. *"Noooo—"*

With a flourish, Mara and Kelly
yanked off the cloth. But instead of the
pile of chairs, there stood . . . the
statue of Simon Plunkett!

Principal Higgins stared and stared.

The audience cheered and cheered.

"It's beautiful!" they cried.

"A treasure!"

"A monument to our school!"

"Yayyyy!"

"But . . . the statue was . . . gone!" Principal Higgins said. "How in the world . . . ?"

"I stole the statue!" said a thin, bearded man who walked out from the side of the stage.

"Mr. Wick?" the principal said. "You?"

The entire audience held its breath.

"Mr. Wick stole the statue with my help!" And Billy Carlson joined Mr. Wick onstage. "He's my grandpa on my mom's side."

"You see," said Mr. Wick, "Simon Plunkett was *my* granddaddy on *my* mother's side. Notice the resemblance?" He leaned close to the statue. The two really did look alike.

"I was happy that Granddad was getting a statue," Mr. Wick said. "But when I saw it, I saw something I had to fix. So I took it."

"If I may," I said. "Goofballs, the clues."

Mara held up the skateboard. Kelly held up the slip of ripped paper. I held up the pencil. And Brian held up the climbing rope, but that made his pants slip, so he looped the curtain rope around his waist.

"These little detectives figured it all out," said the custodian. "We used that rope to pull this statue. We rolled it away on that skateboard. We stacked up the chairs and draped this cloth over them. I thought I could fix the statue before anyone missed it."

"What needed fixing?" asked the principal.

"The statue had bushy eyebrows," Mr. Wick said. "But Granddad didn't have any eyebrows at all. See?" He held up the orange book. It was open to a picture of Simon Plunkett. His whole head was bald.

"How did that happen?" asked Brian.

Mr. Wick chuckled. "When Simon was a boy, there was a fire in his log cabin. He saved his pet badger, Barney, but lost his eyebrows in the fire. I had to make the statue right."

"That's why Gramps asked me for help," Billy said. "So I asked Principal Higgins if I could leave early. He gave me a cool pencil, which we used to keep the Cafeteri-Audi-Nasium door open. Gramps gave me a list of stuff to do. But I dropped the list in the pool when I went to get a mop to clean our mess. The list got wet and it tore when I tried to get it out of the pool. Then, I went to the Cafeteri—"

"Caf!" we all yelled.

"To the Caf and tried to remember the list," Billy continued. "When I heard Principal Higgins coming, I got scared and dropped the rest of the list in the hall."

"Where we saw you," I said.

"I told you it wasn't me because I was supposed to be gone," he said. "I guess you didn't believe me. Later, I went back to the pool to get more mops. I even used one to get the rest of the list up from the bottom of the pool. Everything got pretty wet."

"We heard you splashing," said Kelly.

Billy nodded. "And I heard you coming, so I ran away. I guess that's when I lost the other half of the pencil."

"After that, we went to the kitchen and got the cheese grater to file off the eyebrows," Mr. Wick said.

"And because the grater was right next to the cheese, I took some," said Billy. "I was hungry."

"I needed a picture to get the statue just right," Mr. Wick went on. "When Billy remembered the book in Principal Higgins's office, we went there."

"*We were under the desk the whole time,*" Mara mouthed silently.

"It was finally Sparky who sniffed you out," said Brian, clutching his pants.

Principal Higgins laughed as he went to the podium again. "I think if Simon Plunkett was good enough to start up Badger Point School, he's good enough for us to see him the way he really looked! Thank you, Mr. Wick and Billy!"

The whole crowd cheered.

Principal Higgins then gave his speech. It was long. But it was great.

Everyone clapped. Then he handed out the gold pencils. People loved them. Finally, he turned to us.

"And now, Goofballs," he said, "there's a matter of some water to clean up before we get to the refreshments. But if we all work together, we can mop it up in no time!"

The audience clapped again as Mr. Wick and Billy handed out mops and buckets.

Finally, the curtain went down.

And because Brian had tied himself to the curtain rope, when the rope went up, so did he. And when the curtain came down, so did his pants. Sparky grabbed them. Then he rolled away on Billy's skateboard.

"Wow!" said Brian. "Losing my pants three times in one day. Who would have guessed?"

"Me!" said Kelly.

"Me!" mouthed Mara.

"Me!" I said.

"Us!" said the entire crowd.

Then they said something else.

"Goofballs forever!"

Which is probably how long it will take Brian to get his pants back.